ANCIENT ADVENTURES

BERKSHIRE & HAMPSHIRE

Edited By Jenni Bannister

Years of  Young**Writers**

First published in Great Britain in 2017 by:

YoungWriters

Coltsfoot Drive
Peterborough
PE2 9BF
Telephone: 01733 890066
Website: www.youngwriters.co.uk

FOREWORD

Welcome, Reader!

For Young Writers' latest competition we asked pupils from around the country to step back in time and write an 'Ancient Adventure'. To give it an extra challenge, they had to write a complete story using 100 words or fewer!

The pupils from Berkshire & Hampshire rose to the challenge magnificently. In this collection you'll be amazed by stories about Viking attacks, run from mummies in Egyptian tombs and learn all about Greek mythology. This anthology will take you on a roller coaster of emotions set against a multitude of historical backdrops and, like me, you may even learn a new fact or two along the way!

I'd like to congratulate all the young authors in this collection. Writing a story in 100 words is no easy feat, so well done! I hope you all continue with your creative endeavours.

Jenni Bannister

CONTENTS

Jacob Smith (8) 62
Leo Bailey 63
Lewis Starnes (8) 64
Rhys Brock (8) 65
Aiden Lockey (8) 66
Luca Elliott (8) 67
Charlie Stevens (8) 68
Toby Smith (8) 69
Skye Green (8) 70
Neve Letchford (8) 71
Daniel Verney (8) 72

Park View Junior School, Basingstoke

Kai Wells (9) 73
Kayos Berry (9) 74
Alyssa Dorey (9) 75
Bethany Rich (9) 76
Ryan Sawyer-Angel (9) 77
Daisymae Jones (9) 78
Eloise Sherwood (9) 79
Blake Hadley (9) 80
Kyla Riley (9) 81
Taylier Lawrence (9) 82
Lewis Morris (9) 83
Katie Kirk (9) 84
David Doble (9) 85
Olivia Swinbourn (9) 86
Rylee Scantlebury (9) 87
Lee Galbraith-Wood (9) 88
Charlie Pritchard (9) 89
Kacper Wojton (9) 90
Baden Weston (9) 91
Jeston Witham (8) 92
Mia Towns (9) 93
Zak Merryweather (9) 94

St Mary's Primary School, Southampton

James Evans (10) 95
Sumaiya Sumra (10) 96
Zharita Barwicz (9) 97
Esmat Moradi (10) 98
Pretham Singh (10) 99
Angeli Kaur (10) 100
Ahad Zulfukar (10) 101
Jesse-Jake Le-Warne (10) 102
Eman Bibi (10) 103
Gary Chopra (11) 104
Kieron Patwal (10) 105
Hana Hajji (10) 106
Rahmu Sanneh (10) 107
Naunihal Singh (Luckhen) (10) 108
Mohamed Caynab (10) 109
Reece McCallion (10) 110
Zahrah Maghsoudi (11) 111
Jasmit Singh (11) 112
Yilka Gashi (9) 113
Lara Melo (10) 114
Yamin Ahmed Khan (10) 115
Shaan Mahmood (10) 116

St Teresa's Catholic Primary School, Wokingham

Emilia Casu-Lukac (10) 117
Isaac Hawke (10) 118
Charlotte Reynolds (10) 119
Isabella Jackson (10) 120
Maddie Scott (10) 121
Katie Kelly (10) 122
James Barker-Lopez (10) 123
Oisin O'Shaughnessy (10) 124
Lola Exell (10) 125
Lilly Rose (10) 126
Ben Zacharias (10) 127
Connor Simpson (10) 128

Coen Djamson (10)	129
Lily Ella Grace Smith (10)	130
Kate O'Donoghue-Tolosa (10)	131
Saskia Lipinski (9)	132
Scarlett Sudra (10)	133
Katie Morrison (10)	134
Matthew Cook (10)	135
Alex McLoughlin (9)	136
Rebecca Pye (9)	137
Lucy Stewart (9)	138
Hoel Lagarde (10)	139
Elliot Davidson (10)	140
Oliver Yurek (10)	141
Sam Davies (10)	142
Timur Mirzaev (10)	143

THE MINI SAGAS

The Last Stand

In a forbidden battle with iron on iron crashing together in warrior hands. Arrows set alight with fire in an archer's bow. The forest behind them sets on fire because of a flaming arrow dipped into blacksmith's lava. The fire spreads across the forest, surrounding the battle. The trees burn. Another boat comes onto the shore and it launches water onto the forest. Then a gruesome Viking chops down trees on the battleground and water pours down the hill. The Vikings run to the other boat and eat some food. They've won the battle and they go cheering back home.

Tom Hawkins (8)
Lethbridge Primary School, Swindon

The Secrets Of Max And Frank The Vikings

One summertime, there was a brother Max and a brother Frank. They liked playing Vikings together and watch about the Vikings together.

One day, 'Come on Max, come outside,' said Frank.

'Okay, I'm here,' said Max. Max and Frank saw a portal and decided to go through the portal and entered the Viking centuries.

'Hello strangers,' said a boy called Albert, 'my name is Albert.'

'We know a lot about Vikings,' said Frank.

'Why don't we stay and learn a bit more about Vikings with Albert?' said Max.

'And this is our house,' said Albert.

Rosie Teal (10)
Lethbridge Primary School, Swindon

The Vikings Are Coming

Eric and Scott were sailing to the forest and they were going to search for some buried treasure in the forest. When Eric and Scott found the treasure someone was stood directly in front of the treasure. 'Urrrh!'

'Eric stay back and I'll get the treasure,' shouted Scott.

'I'll challenge you to see who'll get the treasure first and come out with life,' bellowed Ragner who was totally keeping the treasure to himself.

'Bring it on then,' announced Scott bravely.

'Go! I've got the treasure,' howled Scott.

'Quick, follow me to the longship,' barked Eric.

Connor Sherriffs (8)
Lethbridge Primary School, Swindon

The Blood Of The Scots

In a dark, mushy forest there were two warriors called Harold and Olaf. They were storming towards a battlefield. *Crack!* A tree blocked their way. Then they had to think quickly. 'Can we climb over it?' asked Harold.

'Don't be stupid,' laughed Olaf. He had an idea. 'Why don't we chop the tree in half and then push it?' said Olaf.

'Let's do it!' exclaimed Harold. Yes, they did it. 'Now let's go to battle. There was blood everywhere, even on people's faces. Then the Vikings won...

Oliver Staff (8)
Lethbridge Primary School, Swindon

Incoming!

Crash! The Vikings charged towards us. We stood our ground on the battlefield of hope and a legendary battle commenced. Metal clashed and we forced back the Vikings. Suddenly, a flaming arrow was shot with deadly accuracy straight at my father, the chief! 'Incoming!' I yelled.

'Coming through!' he cried.

Hours later dead Vikings lay scattered, clutching their wounds. We had won! That evening we ate roast ham, chicken, beef, gammon and deer and drank blood-red ale while artists painted a bloodthirsty battle scene.

Jack Innes (8)

Lethbridge Primary School, Swindon

Augeeni's Chop!

'You stole my crown!' roared Elizabeth the First, who is the queen. Augeeni stood frozen on the spot. 'Come with me Augeeni!'
'OK!'
'Head Chopper come and get your chop stuff ready!' When Head Chopper had his things ready Augeeni sloped into the prison cell. The cell was dark and gloomy. Later Augeeni was pulled to a chop block. The crowd cried and booed. Augeeni was forced to kneel down over the chop block. Augeeni cried and cried. 'I will think of my m...' *Chop!*

Romi Beach (8)
Lethbridge Primary School, Swindon

Blood Is Victory

It's a deep, dark, dangerous village. One day they received a letter which said: 'There's a battle on tomorrow. Do you want to be in it?'
After the battle was done music echoed up when Ragner's team sang. Then the results came out. It was a draw! The prize was twelve weapons instead of 24 weapons. Ragner slammed the door in anger. 'We'll beat them up!' announced Ragner. Ragner asked Harold's team to stand under the blood-covered hut and it fell down. They got the 24 weapons. Victory had come to Ragner's team. That night they had a feast.

Izzy Hains (8)
Lethbridge Primary School, Swindon

German Attackers

The wind howled as the Germans came over their heads. Grandad, Freddie and Freddimena were scared. German attackers tried to bomb them. It was very scary. Grandad and Freddimena told Freddie not to call the Germans to the UK. 'Freddie come here!' shouted Freddimena.
'No, I need the Germans,' screamed Freddie, but Grandad took Freddie home. When they were at home Grandad called the spitfire company to kill the Germans and the Germans didn't know about it. The spitfire flew right above the Germans and bombed them. They all died so Grandad and the kids walked home.

Faith Lloyd (8)
Lethbridge Primary School, Swindon

That Went Wrong!

The wind howled as the Vikings closed in. An
anchor dropped and war began... 'Charge!' As they
charged the Vikings' swords went flimsy.
'What's happened?' they shouted. The Scots
weren't defended. Everyone stopped dead... The
Vikings had never lost a battle before. 'Come on
guys I don't understand why we were so horrible to
each other, do you?' To everyone's surprise the
two tribes started to hug each other. Laughter could
be heard from miles around. A brilliant story for
history to tell. But is that the end of the story?

Lola Spackman (8)
Lethbridge Primary School, Swindon

The Viking Battle

'Attack!' shouted King Ella, as his longboat pulled up to shore. 'Is that a flaming arrow?'
All the Vikings gasped in fear. The arrow was seconds away from hitting his face... nobody was brave enough to step up to the challenge of saving him. Except that is for the mighty Viking Augini who slammed his shield in front of the arrow. The arrow bounced off the metal shield and hit the Scot's village, which subsequently set on fire. At that very moment a bomb shot across to the Scots. Blood sprayed everywhere, the vicious Vikings had won again.

Isabelle Bowen (9)
Lethbridge Primary School, Swindon

The Gruesome Battle

Death was upon us, blood scattered everywhere. This was a battle like no other... Suddenly, a deadly poison arrow was directed at the king! I was fighting, all the Vikings were fighting. I tried to listen in case an arrow was shot. Something went *whoosh!* It was an arrow! I yelled at the king but he stood dead. I jumped and I... missed! Just at that moment the king was furious! Without warning I yelled, 'There is an arrow heading towards you!' The king received it so quickly but silently the king raised his shield.

Yehia Sarhan (8)
Lethbridge Primary School, Swindon

The Shipwreck

On the wrecked battleship, a gold strike of lightning struck the middle of the ship. All of a sudden the gloomy ship collapsed whilst everyone abandoned ship. The ship sank all the way to the bottom of the sea. Jed's father asked Jed, 'Can you spot any nearby land?'

'Only just Father.' Jed led the whole of the tribe to an island. Everyone clambered up onto the shore. The folk built the Vikings a new ship so they could sail back home. But had the storm actually finished? Another lightning bolt hit the boat...

Jed Davison (8)
Lethbridge Primary School, Swindon

The Norman Conquest Of 1066

When Edward the Confessor died there had to be a new heir. There were three people who wanted the throne: Harold Earl of Wessex, Harald King of Norway and William Duke of Normandy. Harold became king and expected trouble. He gathered his troops on the south coast and waited for William's attack. Nobody came. Harald's Viking army landed in the north. Harold fought the Vikings and defeated them at the Battle of Stamford Bridge. Harald was killed in battle. William landed in the south. William's army killed Harold. Because of that William won. William was crowned King at Westminster Abbey.

Emily Fowler (9)
Lethbridge Primary School, Swindon

Loki Herring And The Longboat Battle

As we anchored into the old, rickety harbour, we heard scrambling and whispering from the shallow water below. Suddenly, muscular, hairy men who didn't come from our tribe clambered aboard and started attacking our warriors. Obviously, our men weren't scared of the stupid English men, but I watched as most of my men got slaughtered. In a flash, a brilliant plan formed in my head. I grabbed my sharp, shining axe and swung it around me to kill the English. Unfortunately, this plan didn't work. Then, flames bulged around the ship. We all dived off as the English were burnt.

Anna Heydon (8)
Lethbridge Primary School, Swindon

The Voyage Of The Treasure Ship

At the coast, where the sun was rising, birds were whistling, a distant ship was getting brighter, Ragner was jumping up and down with excitement and handed Thorfinn a map. As Thorfinn was in the treasure ship sailing away, he announced to Ragner, 'Thank you. I will sail away and bring something back.' When he got to the island Thorfinn filled the ship with gold, pies, chickens, goats, swords, shields, axes and fish. Thorfinn was feeling really mighty when he returned. However, while he was unloading, the treasure ship suddenly collapsed and nobody knows what happened!

Kesiya Aggarwal (8)
Lethbridge Primary School, Swindon

Rainbow Beard Against Warty, Brutal, Vicious Fighter

One cloudy evening a group called the Vicious Fighters ran into all of the Vikings' longhouses to steal very prized possessions. The Vikings started to realise what was happening and a battle commenced. As soon as it started the Viking leader called Rainbow Beard said to his Viking army, 'I am going to use the special sword to kill the warty, brutal leader of the Vicious Fighters.' The leader of the Vikings crept behind the brutal, vicious leader and chopped off his ridiculously large head and the Vikings won the battle once more.

Lily Morriss (9)
Lethbridge Primary School, Swindon

The Vikings

In a gloomy, dark, wild, stormy wood with branches swaying, lights flickering and lightning striking there were shadows. Harold found his worst ever fierce enemy of all in the universe. They all walked with a heart-beating thump. 'Who goes there?' The head realised it was their horrifying enemy who was going to shoot an arrow. Harold and Oswald heard a sharp flying noise like a bird. They foolishly missed Harold and hit an old, damp tree. It suddenly made a crash on them. Harold picked the tree up and it fell on his enemy. Harold laughed horribly with rage...

Molly Forshee
Lethbridge Primary School, Swindon

The Mystery Behind It All

In the bloodthirsty village peace was nonexistent. There was always something wrong about that village. Suddenly, out of the crisp, golden clouds came a ship that took over the waves. It finally halted, the Scots were in it. *Clam! Shuttle! Bang!* They stormed noisily out of the ship. I was scared. I went numb. They charged excitedly. I gasped in amazement! 'They are strong warriors and they have come to fight!' King Scot of the Scots was on the ship too. He went straight to the King's Tower! He shook it! It collapsed right on top of King Scot.

Imogen Hutton (7)
Lethbridge Primary School, Swindon

Untitled

Bob woke with a *bang!* 'Bob, let's go,' whispered the king. Suddenly, he remembered he was in the worn-out Edinburgh Castle. However, there were shadows moving swiftly. Bob realised the king had been taken by the shadows! His heart was pounding like never before. Bob heard marching. He took out his sword. *Swing!* He had to sprint up some creepy and clammy stairs, they were dark. But in a spark the king was there with more guards to fight. *Swing! Swing!* It was as dazzling and dangerous as an electric storm.

Sonny Lowe (8)
Lethbridge Primary School, Swindon

The Longship Wreck

Veldar awoke on the ship and heard loud crashing waves. It was so constant, Harrald woke up. All of a sudden, Harrald spotted a blink of light. It came closer and closer and closer. It shot with wind past the waves. It was a lightning bolt dashing towards the ship. 'Get the shields,' shouted Veldar. They held the shields under the water and crushed the lightning bolt into pieces. All of the pieces got drowned and drifted to the bottom of the sea but one of the pieces got stuck in the boat and the boat started to sink and sink deeper down.

Emily Sewell (8)
Lethbridge Primary School, Swindon

Mummy Madness

The sun beamed brightly, the wind blew wildly. Chloe was in ancient Egypt. Astonishingly, a pyramid was open. She went inside. Tutankhamun was in front of her. He had been searching the ruins for lost treasures. When he clapped eyes on her she ran and ran but couldn't find her way out! Chloe saw light - the exit. 'Thank heavens!' said Chloe, 'I thought I was a gonner!' She sped out of the pyramid wishing she hadn't gone in! Chloe rushed back to the safety of her caravan with the terrifying Tutankhamun running after her...

Imogen Smart (8)
Lethbridge Primary School, Swindon

Bloody Battle

There was a big army of men in green with medals and snipers. *Bang! Bang!* They shot our base, we all heard it. We grabbed our guns and jumped out! We were face-to-face. The men in green randomly said, 'Fly!' There were jets everywhere shooting missiles, army tanks bombing, grenades going off and guns triggering! We had to fight back! We charged. We lost some soldiers, so we brought our tanks as well. The sound was as loud as a hurricane! We'd never give up! By the time the sides were equal the battleground was bloody!

Ravi Patel (8)
Lethbridge Primary School, Swindon

JTSA And The Violent Russians

JTSA (Jeffory The Secret Agent) was spying on the Russians because they had a secret chemical called DCA (Dangerous Chemical Assassin). JTSA saw the Russians take DCA into the train so when they left JTSA put a tracking device on the back of the train so he could track them in his Buggatti Veyron. JTSA finally got to America and he got there before the Russian so he could see what they would do with DCA. Suddenly, the Russians arrived and got DCA out of the train and put it at the top of Chrysler Building... *Boom!* It was gone.

Jack Sharland (8)
Lethbridge Primary School, Swindon

The Dark Forest

In a dark, gloomy, creepy forest noises echoed and trees creaked. There was a dreadful thunderstorm and it made the wind echo through the enormous trees. Suddenly, Velder and Oluv heard a creaking sound. Then Velder saw a stick of light. It was an erupting fire. It was drizzling to Oluv and Velder. 'Shall we make a basket out of leaves and things and bark? Then they got to a river nearby. Velder tipped the water on the fire. It was like a forest rain. Suddenly, it put out the flames. 'Quickly get more water!'

Naomi O'Neil (7)
Lethbridge Primary School, Swindon

My Saga

When Violet was rolling and she heard the waves, she got out of her boot. It was a peaceful village and people. People were skipping joyfully. Violet always said good things. Charlotte was her sister. Violet was nice. Suddenly, Violet saw a shadow behind a wall stealing something precious. It was a thief stealing gold. Violet was rushing back with Charlotte to their home and they told their mother and father so they gave them an axe and they rushed back again. In one throw she chopped her head off and the villagers cheered.

Lyla Kilford (8)
Lethbridge Primary School, Swindon

The Mystery Museum

The fascinated history board stood outside. I charged into the museum and wandered to the Viking section. There were loads of amazing facts and there it stood, the statue of Thor. He was the god of thunder. He was just a statue so I carried on. Suddenly, I heard footsteps... I glanced behind me and screamed with terror. There stood Thor with his hammer above my head. Thor engulfed his enemy - me - and struck a lightning bolt. Thor had a hand loose so as quick as a cheetah I pounced out of the museum, but Thor was left...

Lily Peyman (8)
Lethbridge Primary School, Swindon

A Matter Of Life And Death

I said goodbye. I didn't want to, but I had to. I ran to the harbour, the morning breeze on my back. The journey was rough but exciting. We arrived by Wednesday and got all our armour on ready to fight. We stepped onto the battlefields ready to die. It started! We fought like never before. Both Vikings and Anglo-Saxons dropping dead. I knew I was fighting well until an enemy bolted towards me, a sword in his hand. I ran in the other direction, but he had a horse. A sword in my throat. I was dead!

Rebecca George (9)
Lethbridge Primary School, Swindon

The Battle

The chief Viking strolled down to the forbidden field. It was war! The Scots were already there in the field. The chief blew the horn and his army scattered over. Vikings battled: war began. Arrows were shot everywhere. Blood splattered, blood commenced. The chief was attacked. A warrior saw and the Scots were defeated! The Scots were dead! Every last one lay on the floor, defeated. Most Vikings were alive. The warrior was promoted because the Vikings had won! The Vikings made peace with the land.

Ben Lewis (8)
Lethbridge Primary School, Swindon

Vicious Vikings

One gloomy, dark morning, Alex and Lucy woke up. 'Let's go to the forest.' They went as soon as they could but when they were in there they did not see the worn-out sign. The sign said that they should not go in the forest. When Alex and Lucy were in the middle of the forest, they saw a fireplace. Lucy yelled, 'Don't go near the fire!' but Alex was running round and round. Suddenly, fire sparked! Lucy was trying to think of an idea to stop the fire and it was to run...

Hatice Aydin (8)
Lethbridge Primary School, Swindon

The Viking Times

Thorfinn (the vicious Viking) woke up with the wind blowing in his face and he heard the water down by the fjord. All of a sudden another group of Vikings appeared out of nowhere. They started a fight. An arrow had been shot... Thorfinn felt very sad. He shouted out loud. The warrior looked at Thorfinn and they charged... Olaf shot his shield in front of Thorfinn. Olaf saved the day! Everybody cheered for Olaf, Even Thorfinn did. They had a big party to celebrate Olaf, but did the peace last?

Lauren Smart
Lethbridge Primary School, Swindon

When The Giants Invaded

One morning I woke up and I saw loads of giants outside my house and I felt really worried, so I went to get my son, Thor. I went into his bedroom and he was with his friend Loki. Loki was scared, but Thor wasn't, so we went outside to fight. The giants shot Thor with an arrow and it started a brutal battle, but I couldn't fight all of them. Loki suddenly turned into a huge dragon and scared all of them away. I thanked Loki for saving my life and we lived very happily for many years.

Frederick Logan (9)
Lethbridge Primary School, Swindon

The Viking Run!

I, Milly, was so excited to go on my favourite ride. I could burst out singing about it. I was just about to enter the cart when, all of a sudden, a Viking statue came to life. I ran for my life as fast as I could. In front of me I spotted hedges of green and there was an entrance. I tried to lose him. I came to a dead end. I was terrified. There was no escape. He took me by the arm and I had no idea what to do...

Shannon Harrison (8)
Lethbridge Primary School, Swindon

Mummies

In ancient Egypt when I was in a desert I was walking but then I saw a massive pyramid. I was about to go through the door but I noticed that there were three doors. I didn't know which door to open so I opened the first door. I saw when I came into the first room it was really dark so I got my torch out. When I got it out I saw some statues. Just then I saw something coming towards me, it looked like a mummy!

Finley Colucci (8)
Lethbridge Primary School, Swindon

The Vikings

The Viking period was the most vicious of them all. The peaceful, colourful trees glistened in the sunlight. Then, suddenly, Vikings charged at us. Twenty fierce arrows flew straight towards the chief. A warrior called the Wolf Slayer and twenty more jumped up in the air and created a barrier and the arrows stopped dead. Hoorays and cheers erupted and even hugs. This was a story to be told for years to come.

Charlie Corner (8)
Lethbridge Primary School, Swindon

Trapped In The Mummy's Cell

I was on holiday in Egypt and I saw an old boat. I pulled the lever and it teleported into a mummy's trap. On the wall it said: *You Are In The Mummy's Trap,* but just before the door closed Peck, my friend, pushed me out the way. When I looked back blood was on the wall. 'No!' Peck was dead. Was this the last of me?

Yuva Kantamneni (8)
Lethbridge Primary School, Swindon

The T-Rex And The Professor

One day the T-rex was eating grass and the professor was eating lunch. He heard loud marching coming from outside. He went out and saw a T-rex. The T-rex said, 'Hello I am hungry, will you feed me?' The professor noticed something was wrong. He looked in his red, flaming eyes and said, 'You look bad.'

'I'm evil,' T-rex said. *Roar!*

'Run!' said the professor.

'I'm chasing you,' said the T-rex. He ran.

'Argh!' shouted the professor.

'Roar!' roared the T-rex. The professor hid.

'You can run but you can't hide,' said the T-rex.

'Yes I can,' said the professor.

Mimi Harberd (9)
Mill Rythe Junior School, Hayling Island

Aztecs Temple Pest

Alistar opened the door to the Aztec temple door.
Crash! 'What was that noise?' gasped Alistar.
'Rarh, rarh!'
'I will kill you!' Then Alistar's friend came in. Luke
was carrying a baton, looking around the temple.
'What are you doing?' Alistar asked.
'Killing a pest,' Luke answered.
'Rarh, rarh, rarh!'
'What was that sound?' Then something ran across
the temple. Luke smelt dead fleas then Luke pulled
up a trapdoor and found the beast.

Luke Barrow (8)
Mill Rythe Junior School, Hayling Island

The Confusing Fight

'Left, right, left, right!' shouted the legionnaire as we marched into battle.
I felt for my green bubbling potion inside my pocket.
I didn't know what the potion did though.
'Tortoise!' shouted the legionnaire.
We got into formation then ran into battle. We ran so fast along the dusty orange road that the potion came shooting out my pocket, smashing open like lightning.
Suddenly, a bright flash appeared and I found myself giving some grapes to a Celt named Hairy. Nobody was fighting, we were all making friends and giving presents to one another.

Hollie Phillips (8)
Mill Rythe Junior School, Hayling Island

A Day Of Battle

One dark, cold night the Roman army was camping in Britain. The Roman army leader got out of his tent and told the Roman army it was time to go. They got ready and ran towards the Celts. *Bang!* The Celts were ready. 'George, you go at the front please.' The Roman leader was confident. He wanted to conquer his mission He shouted, 'Charge!' They ran on the battlefield. They battled all night. The attack finally stopped.
The next morning they got up early and got everything ready for another battle that was coming...

Rihanna Jackson (8)
Mill Rythe Junior School, Hayling Island

The Legionary Vs The Slave

A legionary was picking berries and minding his own business when suddenly he heard big bangs! He looked to sea, there was a massive black shadow. He said, 'What could it be?' It got closer and closer. The banging got louder. He realised what it was, it was a slave. He gathered all his stuff and was ready to fight. The slave was rowing to invade England. They battled but the legionary scared the slave away, he ran to his boat. He sailed away. The legionary carried on gathering his things. He knew he would come back to fight again.

Milly Lancaster (8)
Mill Rythe Junior School, Hayling Island

A Terrifying Roar

I was in my warm bed, I couldn't sleep. The wind was howling and suddenly, *bang!* I ran down the creaky stairs and, suddenly, I saw a big brown T-rex outside my back door. I screamed loudly. The dinosaur turned around and roared in my face, louder than ever. I ran into my mum's room shivering in horror. I told her what had happened and never mentioned that day again. But I couldn't get to sleep again. I had a feeling it was coming or more dinosaurs were coming. I looked out of my window. I saw they were coming again.

Lucy Trueman (8)
Mill Rythe Junior School, Hayling Island

The Games

The gladiator swished his metal sword through the sunny sky. He would not be beaten with 100,000 people watching him. The sun glowed on his face as he peered into his enemy's eye. It was like a black hole. All of a sudden a glowing white horse charged out of the entrance. The horse galloped in the mighty wind, its angel-like hair shone. The gladiator stood still like a statue... 'Hail!' the crowd shouted. Julius Caesar stood up. The gladiator was worried. Caesar raised his thumb. The gladiator could live his wonderful life!

Louisa Bettesworth (8)
Mill Rythe Junior School, Hayling Island

Mummy Madness

There were two children in Egypt. They went outside in the desert and they heard some stories by older children about a scary dead person that died and came alive again and had tissue paper wrapped around them. The children didn't believe it. They ran into a cave to explore it. They heard footsteps. Something swept past them. The children thought that thing was wrapped in tissue paper. It made a howling noise. They saw it coming closer and closer. They saw a strip of tissue paper, then another and then they saw the face - Mummy!

Caitlin Shepherd (8)
Mill Rythe Junior School, Hayling Island

The Battle Begins

The wind screamed and ripped the sails fiercely. There was a hill at the side of the river. The legions shouted and screamed, 'Celts!' Drums were beating loudly, eyes were staring from the top of the hill. An arrow hit the wood. I had butterflies in my tummy. Shining and staring was all we could see. I knew who were waiting. They stood in silence. Silence was a bad thing to happen. The Celts had blue prints and strange markings all over their bodies. It seemed like they were ready for war. A spear flew, the battle began.

Tegan Throup (8)
Mill Rythe Junior School, Hayling Island

The Amazing Fight

One gloomy night the Romans geared up, jumped on their boat and went to fight. They went to the battlefield and waited for the Celts to arrive. Eventually they arrived after three hours. All the Celts were working when someone came and shouted, 'Fight!' The battle began, it was intense. The Romans fought with their shields, spears and swords. The Celts used their tools. The two men, Marcus and Claudius, were the two best fighters so they were bound to live. Before long half of the Celts were gone. The rest vanished.

Sophie Neale (8)
Mill Rythe Junior School, Hayling Island

Warp Villain

One day, in Rome, Maximus was paying 100 coins for a new gladius as the one he had was too rusty. He spotted a man with an antique gladius that he stole! Maximus chased after the filthy villain to face him. Then the villain went down an alleyway and Maximus lost him. Before him lay a gravel track and on it lay a dull sword marked with letters I...I...M...E... He touched it and the blue bubble came out and teleported him to a desert. The dry sand meant that he was in Egypt! Ancient Egypt! The soldier gasped in shock.

Jack Micklewright (7)
Mill Rythe Junior School, Hayling Island

The Deadly Battle

There was a ginormous ship sailing towards me. It looked Roman, but I couldn't tell at this distance. I ran back and told the other Celts what I had seen. So we got our shiny silver armour and ran out onto the cliff side, frightened, but bravely waiting for whoever was trying to attack us. In a couple of hours the ship arrived and everyone was suddenly moving at once. Hundreds of men came charging out to invade our land. So now all of the Celts ran down the cliff to fight and to kill and show how angry we were.

Daniel Allen (7)
Mill Rythe Junior School, Hayling Island

The Romans Are Coming!

In a farm there was a Celt called Arthur and a dog called Frederick. One evening, Arthur was farming on a small cliff when, *boom!* An arrow hit the side of his house! 'Fred!' screamed Arthur, 'The Romans!' Arthur and Fred ran to the house. The air was filled with sharp arrows. Arthur's heart was racing rapidly and pounding every second. His friend got hit. Suddenly 25,000 roars filled the cold air. The deafening sound of thunder approached the cliff. The battle was about to begin...

Henry Terry (8)
Mill Rythe Junior School, Hayling Island

The Roman In Battle

One day the Romans were on a boat. Bob, Lily, Marcus, Max and Marly were rowing the boat because they were slaves. The slaves got told to row faster and they also got whipped. All of a sudden they reached land, then they got ready for battle. One of the Celts disguised himself as a Roman. When he started the fight he fought the Romans. The Romans were fighting the Celts using shields, spears, swords and daggers. The Romans got mad at the Celt that disguised himself. They told him off but he ignored them.

Lacee Lawley (8)
Mill Rythe Junior School, Hayling Island

Bloody Mary Pays A Visit

It was a sunny morning when I was in bed, until a shout awoke me. It sounded like my butler's voice, but he was asleep. I jumped up and looked out my window... it was my sister, Bloody Mary, she was coming for her revenge! She wasn't allowed to be queen so she got mad and turned against us! My father woke up and got on his horse, to protect his kingdom from being destroyed by his murderous daughter and her crew! Mary was paying a visit, the kingdom was afraid and so I invited everyone in.

Dannan Simpkin (8)
Mill Rythe Junior School, Hayling Island

The Bullet Of Truth

In a deserted, broken house Harry and Echo were trying to snipe an enemy plane. Echo finally got it in range and shot it down. Then they heard a bark. There was a dog in a house and the plane was going to crash! Harry and Echo ran inside and grabbed the dog. After that they ran out with the building behind them on fire! Then they saw two Germans who ran over to shoot them! They ran into a big building and went up the stairs into a deserted room. Then the Germans caught them and shot a bullet.

Alasdair Combe (8)
Mill Rythe Junior School, Hayling Island

The Murdering Monsters

Lucas and Howler, his dog, once left their house to go to the huge woods to see some deer. When they got there it was dark. Lucas heard footsteps and they were loud. Lucas was lost. He saw Howler run home. Lucas looked around the woods until he saw something, it had big teeth the size of a pencil. It cornered him. It had yellow eyes! Lucas screamed as loud as he could. Lucas ran as fast as he could until he found a cave. Lucas had seen a dinosaur which cornered him but was it real or fake?

Lucas Gannon (8)
Mill Rythe Junior School, Hayling Island

The Monster In The Shadow

It was a dark night. The stars shone in the night sky. The loose pebbles tumbled. I could hear owls hooting and birds tweeting. Then I heard something... It was big. Just then, I figured it was a monster. My heart froze, my jaw dropped. There stood the beast, it had bloodied teeth and hunger in his eyes. It was then I knew I was trapped. I kept creeping out. I could see a big pair of beady eyes staring in the distance. I screamed louder than ever before. Something roared... what was it?

Jessica Hill (9)
Mill Rythe Junior School, Hayling Island

The Battle Begins

One night I was angry so I led my army to a fight. The lightning struck our boat, we were sinking like crazy. We got off in time. The Celts thought we were attacking. We ran towards a mountain, It was like a battleground. We were surrounded by Celts. My Romans died... I could hear the Celts screaming in my face. Out of nowhere I could see a big scary army coming towards me, the armour shining in my blue eyes didn't help in this situation right now... what should we do next?

Harry Croft (8)
Mill Rythe Junior School, Hayling Island

Attack The Celts

The ship was crashing against the humongous waves. Then they finally got to Britain. The Celts were going crazy. They had blue paint all over their bodies. Then the Romans used weapons and fought the Celts until they surrendered. Then they went to invade Italy. They jumped into the boat and sailed to Italy and invaded Italy until they surrendered. Then they went to take over France, then they killed every one of them. Then they went home on the boat and sailed back home.

Jake Ewens (8)
Mill Rythe Junior School, Hayling Island

It Came Upon Me

One hot, windy day, I was floating in the calm sea. It felt like someone or something was watching me. Suddenly, an enormous creature pounced at me from under the dark blue sea. I tried to swim to the shore as fast as possible. But I felt my death coming closer and closer... I realised it had wet scales and bloody teeth. It disappeared back into the depths of the ocean, but I felt a bite to my foot and I started to be dragged below the waves. Death came upon me.

Charlie McGlone (8)
Mill Rythe Junior School, Hayling Island

Dinosaurs

In the morning I suddenly heard a noise. It was a dinosaur. I knew it was because the roar made the trees shake. When I got closer I heard more noise. Suddenly, I saw a dinosaur stuck in a hole. I ran back to the den to get something to help. I knew it was dangerous but I had to do it. When I got the rope I ran into the woods. I pulled and pulled. I got the dinosaur out of the hole. Slowly, we became friends. Just then I saw the fiery eyes of a giant T-rex...

Joe Britton (8)
Mill Rythe Junior School, Hayling Island

The Lost Fight

I was training with the other Romans. After training we searched the battlefield three times for the Celts. We looked everywhere for the Celts. I had a little sit down on the wet grass. After one hour my bum was wet so I stood up. Then we practised the tortoise. The tortoise was a bit hard. Then I saw a pair of eyes. What was it? I thought to myself for a second, *what should I do?* I told the commander. I said, 'Should we fight the Celts?'

Oliver Burroughs (8)
Mill Rythe Junior School, Hayling Island

The Pharaoh Returns

The sand blew in Exoda's eyes. He ran to the River Nile and washed his face. While his face was dripping, he ran to his pharaoh, Tutankhamun, but he wasn't there! There was a new pharaoh called Cleopatra. It was a disaster. He could see the evil in her eyes. She walked to her family pyramid to see her mother's tomb. When she came out she walked quite a distance away. Exoda opened it. A couple of minutes later two yellow eyes looked at him.

Lucy Walters (8)
Mill Rythe Junior School, Hayling Island

A T-Rex Invasion

A caveman went out to find some food. He killed a cow to get food. He came across a volcano, so he cooked his beef. Suddenly, 10,000 T-rexes jumped out. The volcano burst. The bright hot lava came out of the volcano. The caveman ran. One T-rex died, another ran to the caveman's house. The lava spread around the house. The lava killed 100 T-rexes. The caveman saw meteors coming down to Earth. The T-rexes were all dead at last.

Alfie May (7)
Mill Rythe Junior School, Hayling Island

The Howling Fight

The wind was howling, the Romans were going to the Celts. Maximus was feeling brave. They were almost there. They stopped. They needed to go to the battlefield. They got there and climbed and climbed and climbed. Finally they got there. The Celts were coming and they were climbing up the hill, up, up, up and up. Then they went to their side of the battlefield and shouted, '5, 4, 3, 2, 1.' The battle began. They all ran...

William New (7)
Mill Rythe Junior School, Hayling Island

The Great Terror

The water dripped off the large forest trees, they stood tall like statues. The ground was alive with tons of ants. Suddenly, I heard a loud roar! The ground started to shake, so did I. What was it? Quickly, I dashed up a tree in terror. All of a sudden, a tree toppled over. I was horrified. Two bright eyes beamed at me. 'Run!' I yelled. It was a dinosaur with a scaly spine. It was a triceratops! I sprinted for my life.

Jacob Smith (8)
Mill Rythe Junior School, Hayling Island

The Dinosaur

The sun rose up and the sky popped up and then everyone was awake. When it was 12 o'clock Lucy, Olivia, Freddy, Katie and Luca went to the woods. Just then, Lucy heard something. It came closer and closer and without warning it appeared. It was a giant dinosaur! They all made a booby trap for the dinosaur. When Lucy grabbed the dinosaur she tried to spring it back to its home. Then they all went to sleep and had a snooze.

Leo Bailey
Mill Rythe Junior School, Hayling Island

Two Ferocious Predators

Three million years ago there were two ferocious predators hunting for prey in the Atlantic Ocean. Suddenly, out of the corner of the basilasaurus' eye, it saw a megalodon, so the basilasaurus attacked. The megalodon saw the move of the basilasaurus! So as the basilasaurus charged the megalodon slammed its tail at the basilasaurus. It was critically injured. The megalodon swam away. The basilasaurus was slowly dying!

Lewis Starnes (8)
Mill Rythe Junior School, Hayling Island

How I Survived

Bang! Bang! Bullets sprayed on the bunker... I was worried we would not make it. Then I grabbed my gun and *puff!* There came out a huge big shadow! It looked spooky. I tried to get closer then I jumped from the window and I crawled to the turret and started firing. *Pew! Pew! Pew... Bang!* It was gone. Then I got on a chopper and went home. I'll never know what it was.

Rhys Brock (8)
Mill Rythe Junior School, Hayling Island

Untitled

One day in World War II a German commander and his four troops went to England and murdered twenty people. Five of them were children. Then the wind howled over one hundred miles an hour. The rain hammered down and an English general and his six troops came and killed the German soldiers and left one wounded so the German commander ordered a peace treaty. After that the Germans left England forever.

Aiden Lockey (8)
Mill Rythe Junior School, Hayling Island

Untitled

The earth shook. I grabbed my gun and rushed outside. The stink of the trenches made me feel sick. I had no idea what was happening but everyone kept shouting. 'Follow me! We need back up now!' they yelled. Rapidly I shot at the enemy. I'm sure that I hit one or my own men. Suddenly, a puff of smoke came. Straight away I knew what was going on. I was in World War One...

Luca Elliott (8)
Mill Rythe Junior School, Hayling Island

The Raptor Is Here

One terrible day I was on my ship sailing.
Suddenly, I saw a hot, rocky cave. I heard a roar
and I saw brown dust flying everywhere. I saw a
razor-sharp claw. I found traps. It was incredibly
fast. It was a dinosaur! I heard something behind
me. It was there! It tried to gobble me up! Just then
I found a sword. I stabbed him! I was free finally,
but were there more?

Charlie Stevens (8)
Mill Rythe Junior School, Hayling Island

We're Off To Stonehenge

'Let's go to Stonehenge,' I said. I couldn't wait to go there for a trip. Stonehenge is a lovely place to go because of the bright and colourful stones in a circle for us to look at. Me, Aiden and Alfie were thrilled to be there. I couldn't believe it. The stones were glowing in front of our eyes...

Toby Smith (8)
Mill Rythe Junior School, Hayling Island

The Spine Dinosaurs

I was in a jungle. The jungle was very gloomy and dark. The birds were squawking on the trees up high in the blue sky. Suddenly, something came this way! My skin turned white and I ran for my life. It was a spinosaurus! It roared loudly. I screamed out loud in fear! I knew it was too late to hide.

Skye Green (8)
Mill Rythe Junior School, Hayling Island

Saint George's Death

I was on my knees being dragged up the steps. The raging wind bellowed outside. I got closer to my death. I rested my head on the gallows. The locks clicked; I knew I was trapped, I could see the emperor's eyes gleaming with rage. I knew this was the end. The axe came down and *chop!*

Neve Letchford (8)
Mill Rythe Junior School, Hayling Island

The Chase

The wind howled in the cold winter forest. A dumb T-rex was following me through the forest. I stopped at the peak. He came running up but I fell. I was doomed until a pterodactyl swooped me up and put me up on the surface of a mountain. The T-rex fell to its death.

Daniel Verney (8)
Mill Rythe Junior School, Hayling Island

Battle For Life

Long ago a brave Viking warrior, Kai, and his army
went in their boat to war.
Some of his friends were part of his army,
Terrifying Toby and Dangerous Dylan, they had
been friends for ten years and fought many battles
together.
On their boat, whilst paddling, they felt scared and
excited.
Terrifying Toby asked Dangerous Dylan how he
was feeling.
Dangerous Dylan replied, 'I feel very scared.'
Kai shouted, 'Don't worry boys we will be fine.'
He looked out to the land they are heading for, a
puff of smoke appeared. The great war had started.

Kai Wells (9)
Park View Junior School, Basingstoke

Crazy Mat!

Once, there was a Viking called Crazy Mat. He went super crazy. His friends Perfect Pat, Tidy Tom and Messy Mich all tried to stop him, but Crazy Mat couldn't help it, because he had anger issues.
One day Crazy Mat woke up and trashed his room! Then Mat ran away.
Twenty years later Crazy Mat came back, but he was still very angry,
and he burnt the forest! His friends came home and tried to help him with his anger issues and it worked. They had a big party and they never ever, ever had any problems again, apart from the forest! But they were happy and became even better friends!

Kayos Berry (9)
Park View Junior School, Basingstoke

The Great Time Travel

We were whirling through space and time, when BotBot jolted and landed. Our computer flashed saying *Time: 11:56. Date: 02.09.1666.* We stepped outside looking confused. BotBot flashed his green laser towards Pudding Lane. We crept closer and closer and we could smell smoke.

We looked up, 'Up there, up there, look at the oven!' Ashley bellowed. We grabbed our gas masks from BotBot and rushed inside. We ran to the top floor where the oven was smoking, we quickly turned it off. Then we jumped out the window, BotBot caught us.

Alyssa said, 'Another job done and done well!'

Alyssa Dorey (9)
Park View Junior School, Basingstoke

The Horrible Roman

Once upon a time, in a faraway land, there lived a horrible Roman called Isaac, with a nasty heart. He said horrible hurtful things to people. The nasty Roman challenged everyone. 'You think I'm stupid? Let's have a vote on it.'
Everybody agreed to do so. Then something strange happened. Some people decided to vote to say he wasn't stupid, thinking the horrible Roman was definitely going to lose, but so many people voted and he ended up winning.
The horrible Roman gave a nasty grin. 'You thought I was stupid? Now look who's laughing and who looks stupid.'

Bethany Rich (9)
Park View Junior School, Basingstoke

Olympics

It's 776BC and I am training for the Olympic foot race and discus. I am getting up early each morning to run three miles and practise throwing the discus.

It is the morning of the Olympic foot race, I am at the start ready to run. I start running as fast as I can towards the finish.

Later in the day I attend a large banquet. I eat lots of food and enjoy myself with the other Olympic winners.

Ryan Sawyer-Angel (9)
Park View Junior School, Basingstoke

The Greek Olympics

It was a sunny day in Olympia. Out of nowhere an amazingly talented girl who went by the name of Daysias appeared. She wanted to achieve her life-long ambition, participating in the Olympics. Unfortunately she was unable to do so because she wasn't well known and there wasn't enough space for her... Luckily for her another athlete had a fall which led to her being unable to participate. Because of that Daysias was finally able to participate, and take up that space. She not only achieved her life-long dream, she had also achieved higher. She had won!

Daisymae Jones (9)
Park View Junior School, Basingstoke

Gone In A Flash

Amongst the flowers, there were two girls. They were walking through the meadow. They saw this sweet-smelling flower. The smell drew them closer and closer. When they got there and sniffed it, *flash!* Suddenly, they were in a dark and gloomy world. The girls saw men with beards and they smelt of rotten eggs. They were on a longboat. Waves crashing, thunder bashing, horns on their heads, fights crashing together, mammoth coats with scars from fighting. The girls started running as fast as they could and kept on slipping. The Vikings were catching up with them.
'Help!'

Eloise Sherwood (9)
Park View Junior School, Basingstoke

Surviving The Night

'Oh wow what's this?' Dan looked into the doorway of an abandoned base. He circled very slowly and saw a finger bone on the floor. Dan looked up and saw a trail of unconscious people. Dan went to run out of the base but just as he did, a skeleton was standing there. Dan ran back and found a dark room. The skeleton followed and tried to grab him. 'Finger!' called the skeleton. Dan ran and got it, chucking it at him. Dan found an exit, he heard the skeleton shout, 'Run while you still can.'
'I survived!' sighed Dan.

Blake Hadley (9)
Park View Junior School, Basingstoke

Poachers

Gunshots and shouting woke me. 'The poachers were back,' I heard my father say. We lived on a game reserve in Africa and my father was head warden. People kept coming onto the reserve killing elephants, rhinos, lions and apes. Many of the animals were left suffering in pain. Some may take days to die. The poachers don't care about suffering as long as they get their money.
I jumped in the jeep. We raced to where the gunshots came from. Rangers were there. This time they had frightened the poachers away, this time the animals are safe.

Kyla Riley (9)
Park View Junior School, Basingstoke

The Time Machine Mummy

It was on Halloween night. Miss Duke had a party at school. She invented a time machine and then she showed the children. She stepped inside. A naughty boy pressed a button, then Miss Duke vanished to Egypt. She saw a mummy and screamed loudly. She ran towards the time machine. The mummy cast a spell on her. She disappeared.

Back to the school party, the children were dancing. Miss Duke reappeared. She came back as a mummy. All the children screamed. They ran towards the door. Miss Duke cast a spell on the children, they all became baby mummies.

Taylier Lawrence (9)
Park View Junior School, Basingstoke

Greek Olympics

One day it was time for the Greek Olympics to start. There were three people that wanted to win first place. They were James, Jeff and Bob. They all arrived at Olympia, meeting each other as they get there, staring in each other's eyes. Then they all had to do an oath to Zeus. Next they had a long nap ready for the foot race the next day.

It was time for the race. They ran as fast as they could, sprinting as fast as possible. They all ran fast, but James was first, Bob third and Jeff second.

Lewis Morris (9)
Park View Junior School, Basingstoke

The Champion Of Athens

One hot, sunny day in the Greek Olympic stadium, Spartacus was preparing for his big day ahead of him. He was practising the 100 metre race which was part of the Olympics. He began by whizzing round and round the track. *I wonder if I'll win,* he thought.

As the race began Spartacus raced round the racing track. They would have to run around the track five times to win. To Spartacus this was a challenge, because he was against the champion of racing. Spartacus crossed the line. He had gone for gold!

Katie Kirk (9)
Park View Junior School, Basingstoke

Untitled

One day there was a pride of lions. It was 6:30 in the morning. Rex woke up when he saw a butterfly. He gave chase but Rex didn't see the bush, so then he found himself trapped.

It wasn't until much later on that the pride of lions found that Rex was missing. Lock the giraffe was walking nearby when he heard something, and started growling. So Giraffe went over and saw Rex stuck, so started to help but couldn't do anything. So he went for help and more animals came. Rex was safe at home now.

David Doble (9)
Park View Junior School, Basingstoke

Epic Adventure

Once, a dog called Timmy was in his time machine and went to the ancient Olympic Games. Whilst he was there he thought what he wanted to do, he wanted to find out why women couldn't take part in the Olympics. Well he found out why and the reason why was because women were too busy. Timmy spoke to Zeus and other Olympians and made friends with many of them. He took part In every game until it was time to go home.

'I wish I could stay,' said Timmy. Then he went home.

Olivia Swinbourn (9)
Park View Junior School, Basingstoke

The Poor Roman Hunters

Once upon a time there was a group of poor men and they lived in the woods long ago in the Roman times.

One day they went hunting with their bows and arrows. They went further and further into the woods. They heard something. They got their bows and arrows out and looked around to see what it was. It was a huge bear. It took them months and months to try and kill the beast. But finally it came to an end. The beast was dead. They were happy to eat it.

Rylee Scantlebury (9)
Park View Junior School, Basingstoke

Labour 5 Cleans Up King Augeas' Stables

Labour 5 was horrified - he had to clean out King Augeas' stables. They smelt very horrible. King Augeas told us that they had not been cleaned for 36 years with 1000 or more oxen in there.
One day he managed to do it. Hercules diverted tho Alphous river, so it washed through the stables. While he moved the oxen.

Lee Galbraith-Wood (9)
Park View Junior School, Basingstoke

In The Honour Of Zeus!

I am Maximus! I am stood in the hippodrome Greek stadium, hearing loud, expressive and enthusiastic cheering from the crowds. I feel emotional. If I cheat I will be whipped. I throw the hammer and the discus and, in a flash, wrestle my rival to the floor. The mean, tough horses lead chariots to the finish. I am running to the end, the blood is rushing through my veins, distracting me from the brutal cuts to my feet. With huge sweat and exhaustion, I fall to my feet. Have I won? Yes I have won! An astonishing victory, hooray, hooray!

Charlie Pritchard (9)
Park View Junior School, Basingstoke

Greek Olympics

Many years ago I competed in the Olympics. I had lots of rivals who I competed with in wrestling. Once the player that I competed with was much stronger than me but I didn't give up, I beat him which was a real shock, everyone thought he was going to win, but he didn't. I lost in the final but it didn't matter. My friend Maxicus won the 100m sprint race and Badicus won discus. I only won 200m sprint race and got my second loyal leaf crown. That was the best day ever in my life.

Kacper Wojton (9)
Park View Junior School, Basingstoke

How Mummies Were Made!

Once upon a time, back in 260BC at Halloween, there was a party, a Halloween party. A mischievous, naughty, spoilt child called Alexia set up lots and lots of traps to cover everyone in toilet roll. The party was in a week's time. Alexia couldn't wait for her traps to get into action. She giggled every single time she thought about it. However, she did feel a little guilty, but not much! In a week's time was the party. People fell into the traps and moaned, but then it became a fashion!

Baden Weston (9)
Park View Junior School, Basingstoke

The Scary Mummy

The mummy lives on its own in a dark cave in a big forest waiting for its prey to come into his cave so he can hunt them down. The mummy is so scary that nobody will go near him, except for one person called Max. He isn't scared of any monsters, except for a mummy. He is frightened of the mummy because he might try to attack him by biting him. The mummy chases him out of the cave and into the dark, scary woods, he growls at Max. He runs for his life and keeps running and running.

Jeston Witham (8)
Park View Junior School, Basingstoke

What Tomorrow Brings

It's 55BC and we are invading Britain under the orders of Emperor Julius Caesar. We are fighting the Celts. I am afraid I might die. I hear the clinking of the swords and shields and I see blood surrounding me from everywhere I look. The noise is deafening me, I wish I was anywhere but here. All of a sudden I see a Celt rushing towards me. I whip out my sword and I fight to the death. It's every man for himself, I stab him in the heart, I'm safe for now but who knows what tomorrow will bring...

Mia Towns (9)
Park View Junior School, Basingstoke

Beginner's Luck...

One dusty morning, the British were expecting an attack, and the Germans came. German Captain Azker demanded a duel. British Commander Zak declined. However, they began to attack. Many people were killed in battle, even Zak. Both armies were disgraced with their progress, but the Germans had beginner's luck by ending Zak's British reign...

Zak Merryweather (9)
Park View Junior School, Basingstoke

Dreaded Games Pok-A-Tok

The sounds of euphoric cheering made me more competitive.

There was a huge match of pok-a-tok. Starting it was my team The Spears vs The Clubs.

The exciting game continued while we were walking, pulling faces at the other team (the Clubs) to humiliate and distract them, so we could get the upper hand. The arena had vines and rotten leather seats that mice like to sleep in. The game kicked off and we were ahead two-nil and there were only two minutes left before the end of the dreaded game.

'Off with their heads!'

James Evans (10)
St Mary's Primary School, Southampton

Troubles

I was lazily resting bored. Trees rustled and stones flew. I laid in the shade, desperately hoping for some discoveries. Abruptly something else got my attention. Gold glimmered from all corners. Gasping, I seized my chance. It was a heavenly Maya tree! Right from the ancient times. Excited, I lost all senses, foolishly I slipped feeling the agony, my hands stretching out. *Zoom!* I flashed back in time, trudging in uncomfortable rags - then stared at a discarded Maya temple! Soon, I silently started to feast.

'Get out!' a voice faintly whispered. I paused, my blood ran cold.

'Ahh!' Troubles came.

Sumaiya Sumra (10)
St Mary's Primary School, Southampton

The Pok-A-Tok Adventure

My parents died. I wondered how, nobody told me. I kept on trying to find out why. I found out - pok-a-tok. I decided to play the game... As soon as the referee said the rules, I didn't want to play with my best friend (Naran)! Naran lost and I won. Feeling happy I forgot that Naran was being taken away, 'Hedia, help!'

Later, I tried to take him but a guard caught me. We sprinted but it was useless, we came to a dead end. The guard took me and Naran. I heard him screaming. *Chop!*

Zharita Barwicz (9)
St Mary's Primary School, Southampton

Untitled

A story in a jungle involved a man called John and Lloyd his friend. They started to play pok-a-tok in the jungle on green grass which was full of fresh air. John's team scored and Lloyd's team scored as well. That meant Lloyd and John's teams both tied 5-5. They put on a mastery challenge, however they still argued who was best at pok-a-tok.
John said, 'I will be the best!'
'Yeah...' Lloyd said, 'bring it on!' Both were shaking...

Esmat Moradi (10)
St Mary's Primary School, Southampton

Pok-A-Tok Adventure

In the city of Yax Chilian there were two friends, Bimori and Kabil. They were bored so they decided to go in the Pok-A-Tok stadium. Trembling anxiously, Kabil sat down. As he moved the dice his hand froze. He couldn't play. He shouted in panic. 'I can't do this!'

Bimori, with excitement, said, 'You know the punishment - off with your head!' With no time to spare Kabil ran into the jungle and when things couldn't get any worse, there was a dead end. Guards ran towards him with sharp axes and then Kabil knew. It was the end...

Pretham Singh (10)
St Mary's Primary School, Southampton

The Punishment

Stretching and yawning continuously, my eyes drifted to sleep as my family prepared stressfully for the special - but totally disturbing festival. With bells ringing furiously, I woke up to hear my name being called out. They chased me! Not having time to think I sprinted frantically to a nearby rainforest. This was not the best place to go - everything was dry, hot and a bother.

After a few weeks my body was aching and I was in desperate need of water! Was this how my life was about to end, desperate, alone, starving? This was the punishment of the gods...

Angeli Kaur (10)
St Mary's Primary School, Southampton

The Shocking Moment

Pulling my well-stretched clothes, I clenched my wellies and went to do the biggest report in 50 years.

As the days went past, I finally reached the Maya! Looking with astonishment, I was following my trustworthy compass, I finally reached the overcast jungle. I stepped bit by bit. While searching left and right, I smelt the disgusting smell of blood. When searching I bumped my head. Coming back to my senses I brushed the dirt off. Stood in front of me was a temple, searching every corner there were scrolls, sculptures and scripts... Things started to move and shake.

Ahad Zulfukar (10)
St Mary's Primary School, Southampton

Fighting For Her Father!

Wandering in an exotic forest was an adventurous girl called Itzal, alone and worried as her dad had just died. He always said if anything unfortunate was to happen, she'd go to Grandma Bimar.
A tiresome month later... Itzal was sleeping when a loud bang awoke her. Grabbing her handcrafted spear she made her way to the door. A Spanish man was there, so she jammed her spear inside him, but standing broad and tall behind the fallen soldier, was her father. They both burst into tears. 'I love you!' trembled Itzal.

Jesse-Jake Le-Warne (10)
St Mary's Primary School, Southampton

The Lost Mask

I arrived at a place called Central America. A shop was there but it wasn't an ordinary shop, it was a mask shop. I met a man called Kabil.

It was night, someone came into the shop and stole something precious, but I couldn't stop the thief. I got sentenced by the King to look for the precious mask. I got stuck in a jungle. Luckily there was a path to this 'secret' passageway, wow! I went down and found the mask. I earned gold and diamonds for all of that journey I'd been through.

Eman Bibi (10)
St Mary's Primary School, Southampton

Never-Ending Pok-A-Tok!

Running and jumping towards the goal which was my aim, my team scored eight and the opposite team scored seven, my target was that my team had to win. I was feeling exhausted and weary, which made me feel dizzy. I could not let myself down or my team. 'If I'm a warrior, I have to act like a warrior!'
It was ten minutes before half-time, this was the time to show my team that I was a warrior... this was the time to show that I will not be beheaded.

Gary Chopra (11)
St Mary's Primary School, Southampton

The Death

500AD the breeze whistled through gaps in the glowing trees. I marched proudly through the forest but... in an instant a luminous creature paced towards me. Silently I gripped my sharp spear and crawled using all my energy into a garden of reeds nearby. The creature was too cunning... it gripped me with its uncut claws, tearing at my bloodstained mask. Just as I was losing consciousness, I swung my spear and launched it into the jaws of the bloodthirsty beast. *Roar!* I staggered away and the beast was gone. Although I hadn't left the forest yet!

Kieron Patwal (10)
St Mary's Primary School, Southampton

The Maya Terrorism

The sapphire sky glimmered over the towering trees that stood proud and victorious over the Maya. The vibrations of the dancing and singing gave a rattle to the leaf-spilled ground, while the smoke (that came from the fire) filled the forest, in order to scare the devilling-demons that tried to take their very souls. It worked, although something more satanic was going to terrorise the living civilization the soil-filled ground shook once more. A melee weapon shot through the sky, right to the opposite side of the ceremony. There they were - the Spanish... *Bang...!*

Hana Hajji (10)
St Mary's Primary School, Southampton

Amazing Explorer

My name is John Stephen Lloyds, I'm so interested in Maya civilisation. It was a challenge for me to go into Mesoamerica to find out about their civilisation. I only had for a guide some crudely drawn maps. I have been told that they had been wrongly written. I entered into this mysterious jungle city. There was the Mayan city covered with green leaves and colourful fresh flowers. It was a buried Mayan city... I found a pyramid. I also found Mayan number writing scripts. They were amazing people. They were clever people.

Rahmu Sanneh (10)
St Mary's Primary School, Southampton

The Discovery!

I (Jonny Lee) was searching in the mysterious and dangerous jungle for the legendary tribe - the Maya! Whilst I was peering through the reeds, I wondered if they were humans, beasts or animals. When, after a long, exhausting search, I had finally found what I was looking for. A small community were dancing and humming some sort of prayer. Just then... I was spotted! I was chased like an animal... an outsider. Stopping to catch my breath, I tried to swim again. It was too late... I was surrounded by an army of demonic, bloodstained masks... the indigenous warriors!

Naunihal Singh (Luckhen) (10)
St Mary's Primary School, Southampton

The Destruction

Facing the other team in fear, I stretched out for the rubber ball. I, Chel and Chan were on the opposite team playing like Gods (well, they were). Despite our determination, and someone yet to score, Chan launched himself up the ever-lasting wall, (scraping the flesh from his shins) shooting the ball to the ring of victory. The illuminated reflection started fading away, into an obscure sky. *Ding! Ding!* The rumbling ground started to shake in despair. Our team, who were awaiting destruction, shivered as if we were about to meet our end. (Well we were!)

Mohamed Caynab (10)
St Mary's Primary School, Southampton

The Poor Maya

A poor boy lay upon a path, hungry and in need of God's assistance. Without he'd be left starving. He was making a well-organised plan with his friend Seli. They both succeeded, but they'd needed more, it wasn't enough to feed everyone. Polo worried they'd get caught stealing. He decided to do jobs for money to buy food and eat smooth chocolate. In the middle of the jobs he stumbled across an oak tree which may have broken his ankle. But! This did not stop him! He did all the jobs. He earned lots of money for food and chocolate.

Reece McCallion (10)
St Mary's Primary School, Southampton

What The?

With a great shake, I followed as my gleaming eyes pursued an ever-green house - illuminated in gold. One step... two steps... three steps, the long, wiry stairs dropped down amongst the foliage. Stopping still at a particular step below me, on it was the face of the Maize God. I lowered to reach it -
flash! within a blink, I realised I was surrounded by half-naked men with razor spears held in their hands. I turned to look at my bare legs - which were hairier than before; my 'JLS' jacket was now bare skin. I was one of them...

Zahrah Maghsoudi (11)
St Mary's Primary School, Southampton

Zapping To The Past

Staring at Grandpa's invention, I dashed towards it. *Crash!* I tripped over the machine's floor. *Bling! Bling!* The machine switched on. Noisily, the mechanical monster unfastened. Frightened, I walked outside the machine. There I noticed a weird boy shouting, 'Get the ball and shoot it in the hoop!' Dashingly I went to the enemy's team and tried to get the ball but I couldn't get it, because the enemy was too tall. I tried for the last time with a lot of effort. I got the ball off him. Goal!

Jasmit Singh (11)
St Mary's Primary School, Southampton

Untitled

After watching a glorious game of pok-a-tok, me and my friends headed home. My father greeted me with a huge letter, it was made out of rich gold. It was so cool, usually we did not see these kind of letters, so I went for it. I went to the deepest, darkest cave. I'd never been there before. I started the test, my journey. It was serious. I had to answer all the goddess's tests and guess what happened. I passed the test. So I went to meet my goddess and took her place and became one.

Yilka Gashi (9)
St Mary's Primary School, Southampton

Pok-A-Tok

There was a girl called Erany. Her father brought a game called pok-a-tok. They called her friends to play with it. There was a knock on the door and Erany went to open it. It was her friends. Erany was playing pok-a-tok. They lost four pieces. If Erany's dad found out that she'd lost four pieces she would get in trouble. She ran and hid. Her friends took Erany back home and they explained what happened to the pok-a-tok game. They brought another game for Dad. She was grounded.

Lara Melo (10)
St Mary's Primary School, Southampton

The Pok-A-Tok Chase!

Breathlessly I sprinted across the leafy ground as an opposing player (the world's best) hit the ball into the hoop. It was all over! Knowing that I would come to a gory end, I ran as Abbas - a bully - chased me. Losing my breath, I felt like a bear was coming to engulf its prey - me. Rattling the axe to scare me, Abbas, who was filled with fury, slashed the bloody weapon at my left cheek. With blood dripping on my bare chest, I came to a halt. That was it... a dead end...

Yamin Ahmed Khan (10)
St Mary's Primary School, Southampton

A Dead End

Whilst I sprinted through the forest the wind howled. I knew it was going to be a gory ending. I was challenged to a game of pok-a-tok. I was terrified, horrified. I couldn't believe it! I kept on sprinting then I was there. It felt like seconds. *Bounce!* I missed the shot. My jaw dropped. I ran through the forest like I had never ran before. Warriors chased me. The rule was strict death to those who ran. This was it, a dead end...

Shaan Mahmood (10)
St Mary's Primary School, Southampton

Don't Speak Too Soon

The crowd fell silent. 'Welcome all,' boomed William Shakespeare. 'May the play begin!' The actors suddenly appeared like ghosts. Dan and Annika were their names.
'My princess! Thou shalt be mine!' announced Dan. 'Thy slumber may now be restful!'
He flung his torch in the air, not noticing that it landed on the roof. 'Thy sweet...'
'Argh!' yelled Annika.
A brilliant blaze of fire came gobbling up the theatre.
'I have an idea for my next novel... run!'

Emilia Casu-Lukac (10)
St Teresa's Catholic Primary School, Wokingham

Mammoth!

'Ha!' says James. 'You're so funny!' *Thud!*
'Ow!' I hit something big, soft and warm. I looked up. It... it was... a... woolly mammoth! We turned and sprinted. Our fight or flight system started to kick in, we had clammy hands and our stomachs were churning. I looked back, it was gone. Phew! *Thud!* Again? 'James look over... over there!'
'What?'
'A cave with an opening!'
'OK!'
We sprinted like mad men but when we got there, it wasn't a cave at all, it was just the shade, I screamed. We climbed up the cliff face and we ran.

Isaac Hawke (10)
St Teresa's Catholic Primary School, Wokingham

Mummy Madness

They walked across the desert, tired and hungry, with nothing but an enchanted necklace.

'You have to take me to the middle of the desert,' stated a note stuck on it.

Abi and Tom stopped and they saw a shadow rise above them; they heard a loud noise behind them. Tom turned, he gasped. Abi did too. A huge pyramid had risen. A huge door opened and they walked in. They placed the necklace on a table inside.

'Argh!' they screamed as a mummy rose and started chasing them.

It cornered them. They were trapped...

Charlotte Reynolds (10)
St Teresa's Catholic Primary School, Wokingham

Casper The Evacuee

It is London 1940. Casper is 10 and being evacuated to his grandparents' farm in Dunoon, Scotland.

He waved goodbye to his mother from the train, he would miss her.

Three months go by, Casper loves life on the farm, milking the cows, collecting chicken eggs and playing with his best friend Shep the sheepdog

Until one day he received a letter from his mother telling him his father was killed in the war. Casper missed his mum.

Two years later and a knock, knock on the door...

'Mum!' he shouted.

Isabella Jackson (10)
St Teresa's Catholic Primary School, Wokingham

Don't Marry Henry

The black blindfold was tied tightly around my eyes. I could not see anything, not even the tiniest pinprick of light.

I would not be able to see when the sharp sword came slicing through the air towards my neck.

I had been dreading this moment for days: the moment when my head was chopped off... I gulped anxiously - would it be slow and painful or quick and painless?

I could hear the crowd whispering excitedly. I could hear the executioner step to my left, the last thing I felt was the cold sword against my neck, from the right...

Maddie Scott (10)
St Teresa's Catholic Primary School, Wokingham

Hallow's Eve

Hallow's Eve had come again. All were sound asleep, but then... uttered with an awful yelp, which commanded us to help. 'Over, under, in-between! Spread the dirt, leave nothing clean!'
Broom swept out, dust flew high, sand got caught in the batty's eye. Angry bat bit nearest toe, cat jumped and rustled down. Crow took hold of the witch's wig, flew outside to meet the dog which chased after, up they flew, spilled enchanted kettle's brew. Mice were doused! *Poof!* Oh dear! The smell revealed what we most feared, magic brew changed the mice into a fearless Halloweensie crew.
Trick or treat.

Katie Kelly (10)
St Teresa's Catholic Primary School, Wokingham

The Mummy!

As I explored the depths of ancient Egypt, something caught my eye, an unknown pyramid. I leant against a cold brick causing loose pebbles to fall, the brick in the pyramid slowly sank inside... The middle of the pyramid creaked open revealing a large entrance towards a strange image at the back. I silently tiptoed through the entrance, sensing something creep up behind me. The smell of decaying flesh was overpowering - it was a mummy...!

I ran for my life towards the sunlight, outside the pyramid there was a sudden cloud of dust, the mummy had exploded...

James Barker-Lopez (10)
St Teresa's Catholic Primary School, Wokingham

The Mummy

Heart pounding. Legs trembling. I entered the pyramid. All was black, all was silent, but was it? Then I heard a sound. 'Oooooooooo!' I jumped back. As the sweat trickled down my face, I felt something warm and sticky rest on my shoulder. I spun round, it was the mummy... I ran for my life, was the curse really true or was I just dreaming? Then I came to a stop, there was a drop in the pyramid. I had no choice but to jump... I woke up. It was a dream, then I heard a voice. 'Oooooooooo!' 'Hello?'
'Hee hee!'

Oisin O'Shaughnessy (10)
St Teresa's Catholic Primary School, Wokingham

Whoops, Off It Goes

Here we go again, let's just get to the point. So I am a servant at the palace, the toilet cleaner, the least important job. Anyway, who cares?
Henry VIII had lots of wives but one of the main ones was Anne Boleyn. Henry married her and really wanted a son so that he could carry on the tradition from himself. Then Anne Boleyn was pregnant and they waited and waited and waited, till one day she had the baby and it was a girl!
'Off with her head!' he said and that was it, no more Anne.

Lola Exell (10)
St Teresa's Catholic Primary School, Wokingham

The Last Order

Dark, damp, afraid. In a diseased trench, with the constant fear of enemy attacks and death. How could I go on, hating the trenches but dreading to go out of them?

Waiting, waiting for the final whistle. Waiting till we have to go out of the trench and fight for our country. But I don't know if I will survive.

Then all of a sudden, the rest of the army came stampeding out of the trench. Should I go or not? But before I could choose, my heart chose for me and I marched out.

Lilly Rose (10)
St Teresa's Catholic Primary School, Wokingham

A Whale Of A Time

Deep sea-diving... the beauty... the life...! The fish swimming like flowers in the wind. It's a silent place. A magical, mystical stage but don't expect soft and cuddly, expect power, rage, water that chills you to the bone. Unthinkable strength, that can swallow up the invincible, destroy the immortal. *Toot!* Her horn blew farewell. the Titanic was undestroyable and off to America. Mid-journey she strode through the rough protests of the indignant sea. *Rrriiiippp!* The sound echoed through her. Screams and cries ran out. Agonisingly slowly the indestructible sinking, was defeated...

Ben Zacharias (10)
St Teresa's Catholic Primary School, Wokingham

The Unexpected

Tony, 10 years old, lived all on his own with no family and friends. He lived in a town which was destroyed a long time ago. The mud hut, that was his home, survived. He had to make his own food and collect water to survive.

One day he was going to fetch water from the stream. He heard cries of fear. So ran back to his hut as quick as he could to escape impending doom. Footsteps followed him which stopped to leave an eerie silence. The closed door to the hut creaked open and revealed a ginormous shadow...

Connor Simpson (10)
St Teresa's Catholic Primary School, Wokingham

The Mummy

I was exploring the great pyramids of Giza, with two other Egyptologists since there were three pyramids and we were three, we chose to divide and conquer.
As I entered the pyramid it smelt musty and damp. There was no light except the torch I held. I walked until I finally made it to the chamber, the coffins were good but the middle one was empty. I turned around to see a mummy holding another Egyptologist, and then I saw another tomb that he threw it roughly in... I saw the next one with my name on it...

Coen Djamson (10)
St Teresa's Catholic Primary School, Wokingham

Help, I'm A School Girl Get Me Out Of Here!

It's come! The school trip! I was being quite nosy and my inquisitive nature got the better of me, so I went through a 'No Entry' door. I opened the door to discover a hallway that led to a bright light. I saw a huge man stuffing his face with food. The man stood up and bellowed, 'Come here you!' I rushed out. He followed me, but I forgot he could go through walls. He was a ghost! I jumped into a closet. A minute later he found me and said, 'I've been looking for a new wife!'
'Argh!' I screamed.

Lily Ella Grace Smith (10)
St Teresa's Catholic Primary School, Wokingham

The Pyramid That Went Wrong

The wind screeched, the sand rolled on the barren land below as we, the Egyptian slaves, got ready for the disastrous day ahead. Life in these days is very difficult. We Egyptian slaves have to kill ourselves to work. We have no choice.
One horribly hot day, we were forced to create the largest pyramid in the world by demand of the new Queen, Cleopatra. I was helping heave the giant 500kg limestone into place when suddenly the earth began to shake. Everyone started to tremble... I saw a huge block come rolling towards me. That was the end...

Kate O'Donoghue-Tolosa (10)
St Teresa's Catholic Primary School, Wokingham

Jaws!

The wind growled ferociously in the moonlight. An ominous darkness spread in the sky. Suddenly, I heard a noise. It came from the odd figure in the distance.

Within a blink there stood the beast. My heart froze. I sprinted for my life before it demolished its prey. All was quiet; all was still. Not a sound was heard. As the beast approached me I shuddered with fright. At that moment I knew it was the end, the end of me. Before long it approached me. I took baby steps closer then I found I was in the jaws of...

Saskia Lipinski (9)
St Teresa's Catholic Primary School, Wokingham

Where Is My Head?

Henry VIII was married and was going to have a baby. Henry's wife was worried about the gender of the baby because Henry wanted a boy to rule the kingdom and take his place.

Soon Henry's wife had had the baby and they were waiting for the gender. The gender was a girl! Henry got his axe and there went her head. Henry left the baby and started to search for a new wife.

Scarlett Sudra (10)
St Teresa's Catholic Primary School, Wokingham

The Vicious Vikings

The arrow soared through the sky until it hit its target. 'Argh!' screamed a voice. The ground started to rumble, something was coming for her... Vague figures started to appear in the distance with weapons. Was it? Were they Vikings? Just in case, Helena started running. They were getting closer by the minute. *Thump! Thump!* Her heart skipped a beat, her breathing got louder and louder. The Vikings eventually caught up with her; Norbet was furious (Chief Viking of his tribe). Helena froze in fear, sweat poured down her face. Norbet lifted up his axe and swung it towards Helena...

Katie Morrison (10)
St Teresa's Catholic Primary School, Wokingham

Lindisfarne

The steely moon shone brightly. All was quiet and still. The people of Lindisfarne sleep peacefully. The sound of oars slicing the inky water. Danger approaches. The crunch of boots on the shore - swords glint in the moonlight. Shadows move towards the unsuspecting village. A war cry! The chaos of death and destruction begins. The petrifying cries of the innocents. Mothers cling to their crying children. Men battle heroically to protect their simple homes. The ground is stained red; innocent blood seeps into the land, the village of Lindisfarne to be remembered forever. The Vikings have invaded!

Matthew Cook (10)
St Teresa's Catholic Primary School, Wokingham

The Mummy Encounter

Rameses always wanted to experience being in a pharaoh's tomb but he never wanted to experience being locked inside one with no way out, no torch and no way of contacting Mustafa, his Professor, but here he was, locked up by walls of sand and stone. He was beginning to feel claustrophobic and shut in. Rameses heard a shuffle behind him and he turned around only to see the tail of a shadowy figure shuffling quietly away. He turned a corner and gasped. A tall bandage-wrapped mummy staring at him, its ruby-red eyes shining malevolently back at him...

Alex McLoughlin (9)
St Teresa's Catholic Primary School, Wokingham

Boom!

The hostile breeze cackled as it whipped my face. I shivered. Tonight was not the best night for racing around a hill. *Boom!* The sound echoed over the hill. Shots rang in my ears. Heart pounding I turned and ran as fast as a cheetah. I tried to call for help, but my heart caught in my throat! Unexpectedly I stumbled over a tree root. *Boom!* There it was again, this time right behind me. I could feel someone breathing down my neck. Completely terrified, I turned. I felt dizzy. Standing behind me, holding a gun, was a German soldier...

Rebecca Pye (9)
St Teresa's Catholic Primary School, Wokingham

The Black Death

Phew! That was a close one! That's another stinky bucket of sewage I managed to avoid today. The putrid smell in these streets makes me feel so nauseous. I wish my mum didn't send me out here to beg every day for scraps of food. That's when I felt something crawling up my back to my neck. I turned round and there it was! A big, black, menacing rat. Its teeth-like daggers close to my neck. It was the black death! I screamed and ran, not a second to spare, terrified that I had got the plague...

Lucy Stewart (9)
St Teresa's Catholic Primary School, Wokingham

The One Way Ticket To The Roman Times

I skipped upstairs, eager to discover my new, unfamiliar room. I noticed inside a beautifully sculpted cupboard from the Roman times. I opened it cautiously and discerned a vague, gigantic silhouette in the distance surrounded by a large crowd jeering. I cautiously walked in; the sun still scorching my face. I noticed a message inscribed on the right wall: *The Arena of Doom.* Instantly, I realised I was standing in a gladiator arena. Suddenly, coming from nowhere, a huge gladius swung directly at my face...

Hoel Lagarde (10)

St Teresa's Catholic Primary School, Wokingham

The Figure Of Doom!

I was walking home after collecting water from the river. I had a long way to go when the grey sky began to darken. My heart quickened, I started to run; worried that thunder and lightning would strike. I felt the heavy drops of rain and began to run faster. My heart skipped a beat as I heard the first bellow of thunder. A crash of lightning soon followed, lighting up the sky, revealing the outline of a figure in the distance. I froze in fear, a second flash of lightning appeared. In front of me stood a terrifying mummy...

Elliot Davidson (10)
St Teresa's Catholic Primary School, Wokingham

The Battle Of Jutland

The waves splashed our faces so hard it felt like sharp stones. We stumbled on the slippery deck as we carried shells to the six cannons. All I could hear were the vicious dark blue waves. In a blink of an eye, I spotted a fleet of enemy ships. Flashes then filled the sky. In a split second I had loaded the cannon and returned fire. We had already lost thirteen ships. I didn't want to be next. I had only one shell left. It looked like we were done. They fired two shells. *Boom! Boom!* It was the end.

Oliver Yurek (10)
St Teresa's Catholic Primary School, Wokingham

Napoleon

Napoleon was furious. He had lost the battle and had been brought to an island right in the middle of the ocean. His eyes looked like flames. His skin turned red of anger. He felt hate come up in him. He had lost his country, he had lost the whole of Europe! His once so powerful kingdom had fallen down, but one day he would get revenge, one day...

Sam Davies (10)
St Teresa's Catholic Primary School, Wokingham

The Loch

The placid waves didn't harm my hardy boat. What's that? My boat rocked ominously. I caught a sight of a hump of land or life in the sea. Was the monster real? Without all my strength I rowed towards it. It was real... Its gaping mouth opened over me...

Timur Mirzaev (10)
St Teresa's Catholic Primary School, Wokingham

Years of YoungWriters

YOUNG WRITERS INFORMATION

We hope you have enjoyed reading this book – and that you will continue to in the coming years.

If you're a young writer who enjoys reading and creative writing, or the parent of an enthusiastic poet or story writer, do visit our website www.youngwriters.co.uk. Here you will find free competitions, workshops and games, as well as recommended reads, a poetry glossary and our blog.

If you would like to order further copies of this book, or any of our other titles give us a call or visit **www.youngwriters.co.uk**.

Young Writers
Remus House
Coltsfoot Drive
Peterborough
PE2 9BF

(01733) 890066
info@youngwriters.co.uk